Honey
the Candy
Fairy

For Roisin and Alfie Starky-Oakley,
with love

Special thanks to
Sue Mongredien

No part of this work may be reproduced, stored in a retrieval
system, or transmitted in any form or by any means, electronic,
mechanical, photocopying, recording, or otherwise, without written
permission of the publisher. For information regarding permission,
write to Rainbow Magic Limited c/o HIT Entertainment,
830 South Greenville Avenue, Allen, TX 75002-3320.

ISBN 978-0-545-22171-9

Text copyright © 2005 by Rainbow Magic Limited.
Illustrations copyright © 2005 by Georgie Ripper.

Originally published as *Honey the Sweet Fairy* by Orchard U.K. in 2005.

All rights reserved. Published by Scholastic Inc., 557 Broadway,
New York, NY 10012, by arrangement with
Rainbow Magic Limited.

12 11 10 9 8 7 6 5 4 3 2 1   10 11 12 13 14 15/0

Printed in the U.S.A.   40

First Scholastic Printing, July 2010

Honey
the Candy
Fairy

by Daisy Meadows

SCHOLASTIC INC.

New York   Toronto   London   Auckland
Sydney   Mexico City   New Delhi   Hong Kong

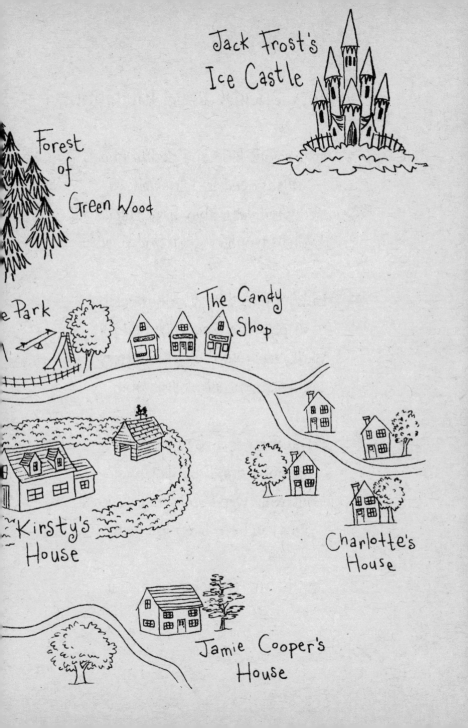

A Very Special Party Invitation

Our gracious king and gentle queen
Are loved by fairies all.
One thousand years they have ruled well,
Through troubles great and small.

In honor of their glorious reign
A party has been planned.
We'll celebrate their anniversary
Throughout all of Fairyland.

The party is a royal surprise,
We hope they'll be delighted.
So pull out your wand and fanciest dress . . .
For *you* have been invited!

RSVP: THE FAIRY GODMOTHER

Contents

A Trip to the Candy Shop

It was a beautiful, sunny day, and Mr. and Mrs. Tate had set the table for lunch outside in the yard. As Kirsty and her best friend, Rachel Walker, sat down to eat, Mrs. Tate suddenly groaned.

"I knew there was something else I meant to get from town this morning," she cried. "Toffees for Gran! I promised I'd take her some tonight, and I completely forgot to buy them."

Kirsty put down her sandwich. "Don't worry, Mom. We can go to Mrs. Twist's Candy Shop after lunch for you," she suggested. She glanced at Rachel. "What do you think?"

"Sure," Rachel said. "I always have time to go to the candy store!"

The two girls smiled at each other. Rachel was staying with the Tates

for a whole week. She and Kirsty had met when their families vacationed on Rainspell Island, and they had been best friends ever since. Somehow, whenever the girls got together, they always seemed to have the most wonderful adventures—fairy adventures!

"That reminds me," Mr. Tate said. "I saw in the local newspaper that Mrs. Twist is retiring. Her daughter's taking over the candy store starting tomorrow. Since this is her last day, Mrs. Twist is throwing a party for all her customers." He winked at Kirsty and Rachel. "I read something about there being lots of free candy, too!"

Kirsty nudged Rachel. "Candy *and* a party," she repeated. "How exciting!"

"We love parties," Rachel agreed, with a grin.

The two friends shared a special secret. They had been busy all week helping the Party Fairies of Fairyland! The fairies were preparing a surprise celebration for the fairy king and queen's 1000th anniversary — but mean Jack Frost had plans to throw his own party the same day. All week, he'd been sending his goblins into the human world to ruin people's parties. Whenever a Party Fairy zoomed in to save the day, a goblin would try to steal

her magic party bag and take it to
Jack Frost.

Kirsty and Rachel had been helping
the Party Fairies outsmart the goblins,
but they knew their work wasn't done
yet. Not if Jack Frost had anything to
say about it!

After lunch, Mrs. Tate gave the girls
some money for the toffee, and they set
out for the candy store.

As they turned onto High Street,
they saw that a few kids were already
crowded outside Mrs. Twist's
shop. But as they came
closer, Kirsty and
Rachel realized that
something was wrong.

A boy was making a

face as he licked a lollipop. And one little girl started to cry. "This candy tastes funny!" she wailed. Kirsty and Rachel went into the shop, wondering what was going on. The tiny store looked very festive. Colorful balloons hung from the ceiling, and party streamers were twisted around the big jars of candy that lined the shelves. Mrs. Twist stood behind the counter as usual—but Kirsty noticed immediately that she didn't look as cheerful as she usually did.

"Hello, Mrs. Twist," Kirsty called. "Is everything all right?"

Mrs. Twist shook her head sadly. "Not really," she replied. "It's my last day. I was hoping to have a wonderful party, but all my candy is spoiled!"

A Sweet Surprise

As Kirsty and Rachel looked around, they could see what Mrs. Twist meant. The saltwater taffy that she was trying to shake from its jar had become one big, sticky lump. The chocolate bars were soft and soggy as if they'd been left out in the sun. And the sour balls were so sour that no one would eat them!

Rachel nudged Kirsty. "Look!" she said in a low voice, pointing at one of the shelves.

Kirsty looked and saw a box of chocolate mice. They all had their paws over their eyes as if they were scared of something. The gingerbread men looked worried, too — they were all holding hands. And, to Kirsty's surprise, a group of gummy worms in a jar were slithering around and actually hissing like snakes!

She quickly pushed
the jar of worms to
the back of the
shelf before
anyone else
noticed.

"Something very
weird is going on,"
Rachel whispered. Just
then, the two friends heard
a chorus of high-pitched squeaks come
from a package of chocolate bunnies.

Kirsty nodded. "It's got to be a goblin!"
she whispered back.

Mrs. Twist put down the jar of taffy,
and pulled out a tray of chocolates
instead. Then she sighed. "Oh, no! What
happened to these?"

Rachel and Kirsty went over to look.

The chocolates had all melted on the tray, and right in the middle was a big hollow spot where something had pressed into the soft chocolate. Rachel nudged Kirsty. She recognized the shape in the melted chocolate immediately — it was a goblin footprint!

The girls exchanged glances. Kirsty looked at the floor. "If the goblin has chocolate all over one foot . . ." she muttered to Rachel.

". . . he'll have left footprints everywhere," Rachel added in a low voice. Then she pointed down at the floor. "Just like those!"

The girls quietly slipped away from the store counter to follow the chocolate-footprint trail. It seemed to lead to a door at the back of the store.

"This is the door to Mrs. Twist's stockroom," Kirsty whispered to her friend. "We can't just sneak in there without asking."

Rachel bit her lip. "Well, we can't just say, 'Excuse me, Mrs. Twist, we think there might be a goblin in your stockroom,' either."

CRASH! Both girls jumped as they heard a loud noise from the other side of the door.

"Oh, no! It sounds like the goblin's making a mess in there," Rachel whispered.

Before Kirsty could reply, she heard Mrs. Twist saying, "This is no good. I can't give people this candy. I'll have to get new candy from the stockroom."

"No!" Kirsty cried immediately. She couldn't let Mrs. Twist go in there — not with a sneaky goblin on the loose! "I mean, um . . ." she searched for words, as Mrs. Twist looked at her in surprise. "You shouldn't leave the shop, Mrs. Twist. Rachel and I will get the candy for you."

Mrs. Twist smiled. "Thank you, dear," she said gratefully. "Bring out anything that looks good to you."

Kirsty nodded and carefully pushed
open the stockroom door. As both girls
peeked into the room, they gasped
in horror. Bottles and jars had been
knocked over, and there was candy
scattered all across the floor. But, worst
of all, there was a tiny fairy struggling

to hold on to her magic party bag, and there was a grinning goblin who was fighting to tug it out of her hands!

"It's Honey the Candy Fairy!" cried Kirsty. "And she's in trouble!"

Goblin Trouble

At once, Kirsty and Rachel slipped
inside the stockroom and shut the door
behind them.

Honey was wearing a pale yellow
dress and lemon-drop-yellow shoes. Her
golden-brown ponytail swung back
and forth as she tried to save her party
bag. "Oh, girls, please help me!" she

cried as she saw the friends.

"Of course we will," Rachel called back fiercely. Her gaze fell on a large jar of candy. "Jawbreakers!" she exclaimed, unscrewing the lid. "Over here, Kirsty." Both girls took handfuls of the jawbreakers and began pelting the goblin with the hard, round candy.

"Ouch!" yelled the goblin, as a jawbreaker bounced off his long nose. He threw up his arms to protect his face—and let go of the party bag. But he released it so suddenly that Honey shot backward into one of the shelves. The wind was knocked out of her, and she dropped her precious party bag!

"Oh, no!" Honey gasped as shimmering golden fairy dust tumbled out of the bag in a shower of sparkles. The girls and Honey rushed to scoop up the magic dust that was shaped like tiny hard candies, but the goblin was already there, grabbing big glittering handfuls.

"Just what Jack Frost wanted," he gloated, stuffing it into his pockets. "Now that I've got this fairy dust, his party will be better than ever!"

"Oh, no, it won't!" Kirsty shouted, grabbing a giant striped candy cane from the floor. Rachel did the same, and the two girls started poking the goblin in the ribs with them. "Ooh! Ah! Ha ha ..." the goblin giggled helplessly, as the canes tickled him. "Stop! Stop it!"

The goblin was laughing so hard that he lost his balance. He stumbled and skidded on the jawbreakers that were all over the floor. "*Whoaaaa!*" he cried, his arms flailing. And then, "*OW!*" He fell over.

All of the fairy dust bounced out of
the goblin's pockets as
he landed. The dust
started to vanish right
before his eyes! The
goblin stretched out
his green hand to
grab it again, but
Honey was too quick
for him. She waved her
wand at the candy canes
and muttered some
magical words.

Kirsty and Rachel
watched in delight as all the
candy canes on the floor started
to shimmer with a golden glow.
Then they stood up and marched in
time over to the goblin.

Before he could get his hands on any of the vanishing fairy dust, the striped canes began nudging him across the room. "Hey!" the goblin protested, as the canes pushed him backward. "Stop that!" But Honey's magic was too strong for him. The dancing candy canes herded the grumbling goblin right out the back door of the store. "That got rid of him!" Rachel laughed, as the door swung shut behind the goblin.

"Phew." Honey sighed with relief, smiling at the girls. Then she fluttered down to look at her party bag, and the smile dropped from her face. "Oh, no!" she cried. The fairy dust had all disappeared, and the bag was empty.

Kirsty glanced around the stockroom. It was a huge mess. There were all kinds of candy on the floor, and jars were turned over on every shelf. "We'd better clean this up before Mrs. Twist sees it," she said nervously. "It's going to take forever."

"If only I had some fairy dust, I could fix everything," Honey said, sighing. "But that horrible goblin made me spill it all."

"Girls!" came Mrs. Twist's voice from the store. "Is everything all right in there?"

"Um, yes! We're coming," Kirsty called back quickly. The girls looked at each other in panic. They could hear the shop bell jingling as even more customers came in to buy something sweet.

What were the girls going to do?

A Flying Visit

Honey thought fast. "We'll have to go to
Fairyland and get new candy," she said.
"I've made a ton for the anniversary
party—you can have some of it. And I
can refill my party bag with fairy dust
while we're there, too."

Rachel bit her lip. "Do we have time?"
she asked. "Mrs. Twist needs the candy
right now."

"Don't worry," Honey assured her. "Once we've got the new candy, I'll send you both back here with magic. It'll seem like no time has passed at all."

"Fabulous!" Kirsty smiled. "What are we waiting for?"

Honey waved her wand over the girls, and amber sparkles swirled around them. There was a wonderful smell of honey, and the girls felt themselves shrinking. 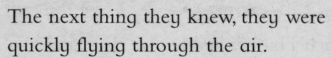 The next thing they knew, they were quickly flying through the air.

"Here we are," came Honey's silvery voice a moment later. "Fairyland!"

Kirsty and Rachel blinked and looked
around. They were the same size as
Honey now — and best
of all, they each had
a pair of glittery
fairy wings! Rachel
smiled with delight
and gave her
wings a quick
flutter.

Meanwhile,
Kirsty was gazing
at the magnificent
golden castle that stood before
them. Balloons and streamers fluttered
from its towers, and joyful music floated
from its windows on the breeze. There
was the most delicious smell of cakes
baking, too.

"Wow!" exclaimed Rachel. "Who lives here?"

"Nobody lives here!" Honey giggled. "This is our Party Workshop."

Kirsty's eyes widened. "Bertram showed us some of the inside, but I never realized the outside looked so pretty," she said. "Still, I guess we are in Fairyland. I should have known it would be beautiful," she added happily.

Honey pushed open a golden gate. "This way," she called.

The girls followed her into the castle.

"This is Cherry's bakery," Honey told them, as they walked through a large, sunny kitchen.

Kirsty licked her lips. There were trays and trays of yummy chocolate cakes, strawberry tarts, cheesecakes, blueberry muffins, and lots more. Some fairies were carefully mixing ingredients, while others were icing the cakes with intricate royal designs.

"Look!" Rachel gasped suddenly. "There's the goblin who ruined your birthday cake, Kirsty. I'd forgotten that the Fairy Godmother had sent him here."

The girls watched as the goblin carefully squeezed pretty icing flowers onto a cake. "And to think he spent all that time messing up cakes," Kirsty whispered to Rachel. "Actually, he's very good at making them look beautiful!"

Cherry the Cake Fairy fluttered over. "I thought it was you two!" She smiled, pressing warm fruit tarts into the girls' hands. "Try these. They're made from my new recipe, with fairy blackberries."

"Thank you," Kirsty replied, watching the fairy blackberries glitter with a magical purple light. *They almost look too good to eat,* Kirsty thought. *Almost.*

"Yum," Rachel said, with her mouth full. "This is the most delicious fruit tart I've ever tasted."

Kirsty took a bite and closed her eyes happily as the juicy fairy blackberries melted in her mouth.

Then Honey led the girls to another huge room, filled with brightly-colored balloons. There were twinkling lights strung all over the high, arched ceiling, and shining silver streamers twirling in the air. But best of all was the fountain of

glitter in the middle of the room, which
sparkled in all the colors of the rainbow.
Fairies were collecting the glitter in pots
and then stacking them to one side, while
Grace the Glitter Fairy fluttered around,
organizing her helpers.

As soon as she saw the girls, she winked
and waved her wand at them, sending a
swirl of pink glitter shooting toward them
in the shape of a heart.

Rachel and Kirsty smiled and waved,
then followed Honey through another
door. They found themselves
on a golden balcony,
overlooking a grand
ballroom.

"We saw this room
when Bertram
visited us," Kirsty
remembered.
"Look, there's
Melodie the
Music Fairy—
and the frog
orchestra!"

The girls couldn't help but smile to see
so many frogs dressed in fancy red vests
and playing their musical instruments.

"There's Bertram," Rachel whispered, giving him a wave. Bertram was so excited to see the girls that he tooted his bugle at all the wrong times in "Happy Anniversary", as he tried to wave back.

Kirsty suddenly noticed that there was somebody else in the great hall, too—the Fairy Godmother. The girls held their breath as she flew over to greet them.

"Hello again, girls," she smiled. "Have you and Honey been having goblin trouble, by any chance?"

"You could say that," Honey agreed. She told the Fairy Godmother what had happened in Mrs. Twist's candy shop.

The Fairy Godmother giggled. "Those tricky goblins!" she said. "Well, you should take some magic candy to Mrs. Twist. That will make her customers happy again."

"Thank you," Kirsty replied, her eyes shining.

The Fairy Godmother's eyes twinkled as she looked at the girls' happy faces.

Then she lifted her wand and waved it over their heads. "Fly, fairies, fly!" she said. "And keep up the good work."

Rachel was just about to reply when she felt herself swept up in a warm, magical breeze. It lifted both girls off the ground and whisked them through the air. The Fairy Godmother waved as they drifted away.

Honey laughed. She was caught up in the rush of air, too. "It's a magical wind," she cried in delight. "A special fairy breeze that will take us to the Candy Factory!"

Treats Galore!

The breeze whisked them along the
balcony and into another room, where
the girls recognized Jasmine the Present
Fairy. She was wrapping gifts in
sparkling paper, with long, silky ribbons
that tied themselves in perfect bows.

Rachel turned herself around with

her fairy wings so that she could watch Jasmine at work. "How do those ribbons do that?" she asked in awe.

Jasmine smiled as the breeze took the girls past her. "Fairy dust," she replied, sprinkling some over a pretty pink ribbon. Immediately, the ribbon flew toward Rachel and tied itself neatly around her ponytail.

"Thank you!" Rachel called as the breeze pushed her on.

In the next room, Phoebe the Fashion Fairy was hard at work, surrounded by rolls of glittery fabric, boxes of shiny sequins, and rows of sparkling buttons.

There were racks of gowns and outfits in every color imaginable.

Phoebe called out a cheerful hello — and the shiny golden ball gown she was working on lifted an arm and waved, too!

Kirsty laughed and waved back. "This is the most exciting place in the world!" she declared. And then she jumped in surprise as the breeze carried them into a very busy room.

Fairies were dashing all over the place. They were trying to catch a shiny silver package with small pink wings as it zoomed around the room.

"This is Polly the Party Fun Fairy's room," Honey told the girls, as Polly flew over, smiling.

"This is my new game—Pass the Magic Present," Polly explained.

"Fun!" Rachel laughed.

But Kirsty shrieked and ducked, because the mischievous package had come flying straight at her! She flapped her wings to get out of the way of the laughing fairies who were chasing the present.

"Bye, Polly," Honey called, catching Kirsty's hands and pulling her toward a pair of bright red doors. "It's my department next—the Candy Factory," she announced. The breeze carried the girls and Honey through the doors and out into a sunlit courtyard. Then, the magical wind went away just as suddenly as it had appeared. When it did, the girls were gently set down on the ground again.

Honey led them along a path to a small orchard. Kirsty and Rachel stared in wonder—the trees seemed to be sparkling!

"Sugar frosting," Honey told them with a grin. She broke off a handful of glittering green leaves. "Here, try these."

Kirsty and Rachel bit into the sugared

leaves, which tasted like sweet, tangy limes.

"Yummy!" Rachel declared, licking her lips.

"There are caramel apples growing on those trees," Honey said, pointing. "And lemon drops over there." They all watched as a couple of fairies flew close to the trees, picking the treats and putting them in golden baskets.

Farther along, Rachel spotted some other fairies using long strips of licorice as jump ropes. "What are they doing?" Rachel asked.

"Strength testing," Honey told her. "And making sure the licorice is stretchy enough." She smiled. "Besides, licorice always makes the best jump ropes. You should try it sometime." The next fairy they saw was making bonbons bounce in and out of a huge jar of pink icing. Fluffy, pink cotton candy flowers grew at her feet, while chocolate mice ran around squeaking.

Honey filled her party bag with golden
fairy dust from a bubbly sugar fountain,
then she took the girls to her own
stockroom. It was piled high with
boxes and jars of fairy candy. "Let's
see . . . Fizzy Fairies, Strawberry Sparkles,
Peppermint Pops, Chocolate Bubbles . . ."
Honey mumbled, loading boxes into the
girls' arms.

"May we have some toffee, too, please?" Kirsty asked, suddenly remembering the errand her mom had sent her on. It seemed like such a long time ago!

"Of course!" Honey smiled. She waved her wand, and a jar of toffee appeared

on top of Kirsty's pile.

"Fantastic," Rachel exclaimed, looking at all of the amazing candy in her hands. "Now Mrs. Twist is going to have a wonderful party for her last day!"

Home, Sweet Home

"Time for me to take you home to
your own world," Honey said, once
the girls' arms were full. She waved her
wand again. Rachel and Kirsty found
themselves surrounded by amber sparkles.
Fairyland seemed to melt away before
their eyes, there was a delicious smell of
honey, a whirl of colors, and then . . .

"Girls? Have you found the candy?"
Mrs. Twist was calling.

Honey, Rachel, and Kirsty were back
in the stockroom of the candy store. And
the girls were back to their normal size,
too.

"Coming!" Kirsty called, out of breath.

"I'll just clean up this mess before I
go," Honey said. She pulled a handful
of fairy dust from her party bag and
threw it into the air. For a moment, the

whole stockroom glowed with golden light—and then the fun began! The gummy worms started wiggling their way back to their jar. The jawbreakers bounced into their jar and whizzed around inside it with a noisy rattle. The gingerbread men hopped into their box, one by one.

As soon as all the jars and boxes were full, they flew back onto the shelves and lined up neatly.

Kirsty realized her mouth was wide open as she watched the fairy magic at work. "I wish I could borrow your fairy dust to clean up my bedroom," she joked. "Honey, that was amazing!"

Honey gave a little curtsy in midair, then flew over to hug both girls good-bye. "I have to go back to Fairyland now," she said. "But thank you for saving me and my party bag from the goblin."

"And thank *you* for all this fabulous candy," Rachel replied.

"We'll see you again at the anniversary party," Kirsty added.

Honey looked serious for a moment.

"As long as those goblins don't mess everything up," she said. "Good-bye!" And with a final twirl of her wand and a stream of golden sparkles, she was gone.

Kirsty breathed in the smell of honey, which was all that remained of their fairy friend. She hated saying good-bye.

"Come on," Rachel said, seeing Kirsty's wistful face. "Let's take these to Mrs. Twist."

The two girls staggered through the door to the shop with all their Fairyland goodies.

"Goodness, you can carry a lot!" Mrs. Twist exclaimed. "Now, let's see . . ." She gave one of the jars a long look. "Fizzing Fairies?" she read aloud. "I don't remember ordering these." She unscrewed the lid to find lots of fairy-shaped treats, all beautifully wrapped.

"Can I try one, please?" a little girl asked shyly.

"Of course," Mrs. Twist said with a smile. She raised her eyebrows as she passed the jar around. "Don't they smell delicious? I think I'll try one myself."

Kirsty elbowed Rachel in delight. She was sure she'd just spotted the fairy on the label giving them both a wink. And as the girls looked closer, they realized that all of the Fizzing Fairies were in the shapes of their magical friends, the Party Fairies.

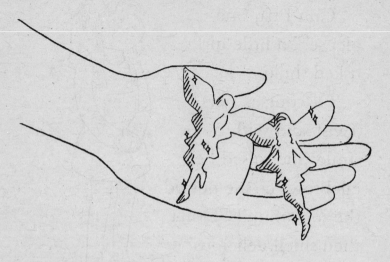

"Mmmmm," all the boys and girls said, licking their lips as Mrs. Twist opened up more of the anniversary party treats. "This is the best candy ever!"

Kirsty and Rachel agreed. The marshmallows were soft and fluffy. The licorice was stretchy and chewy. And the lemon drops were scrumptiously tangy.

"Freshly picked this morning," Rachel joked in a low voice.

Kirsty felt something rustle in her pocket. She put her hand in to find a small bag of toffee, carefully tied with a curly gold ribbon. There was a sticker of a honeybee on the front of the bag. And on the label—in gold, shimmering writing—Kirsty

Made with love and honey in Fairyland.

read the words "Made with love and honey in Fairyland."

"Wow," Kirsty said. Then she smiled. "I think we'd better take these home before I start eating them. Don't they look delicious?"

The two friends said good-bye to Mrs. Twist and left the store.

"That was the tastiest trip to Fairyland yet!" Rachel commented.

Kirsty nodded happily. "Just three days left until the anniversary party," she said. "I can't wait!"

"I hope we get to play Pass the Magic Present," Rachel added, laughing

as she remembered Polly's game.

Kirsty laughed, too. "One thing's for sure," she said, as she popped a lemon drop into her mouth. "We're definitely going to have *sweet* dreams tonight!"

Cherry, Melodie, Grace, and Honey
have their magic party bags back.
Now Rachel and Kirsty need to help

Polly
the Party Fun Fairy!

Join their next adventure
in this special sneak peek. . . .

Woodland Fun

"Good-bye, Mom!" Kirsty Tate called, waving from the school bus packed with Explorers as it pulled away from the school.

"Good-bye, Mrs. Tate!" Rachel Walker, Kirsty's best friend, shouted. She was waving, too.

As the school bus made its way through

the village, Rachel turned to Kirsty.

"Isn't it great that your Explorers leader is letting me come to your mini-jamboree?" she said happily.

"Well, you *are* staying with me this week, so there's no way I'd leave you behind!" Kirsty laughed. "And you're an Explorer, too, even if you're not in our troop."

Rachel nodded. Both she and Kirsty were wearing their Explorer uniforms. "I'm really looking forward to this," she said eagerly. "What did you do last year?"

"We met up with another troop of Explorers—just like we're doing this time—so there were lots of us," Kirsty explained. "We played games, ran races, and there were prizes. Then we roasted marshmallows around the campfire." She grinned. "It really was just a big party in the woods!"

Rachel's eyes opened wide. "A party?" She gasped. "You know what that means."

Kirsty clapped a hand to her mouth. "Oh, I didn't realize!" she said. "We'll have to be on the lookout for goblins. . . ."

"Yes, we'll have to keep our eyes open," agreed Rachel, as the school bus came to a stop in a large clearing in the woods. There were already lots of Explorers milling around. The other troop had arrived! "We can't let the goblins steal any of the Party Fairies' magic bags," she added firmly.

RAINBOW magic™

There's Magic in Every Series!

The Rainbow Fairies

The Weather Fairies

The Jewel Fairies

The Pet Fairies

The Fun Day Fairies

The Petal Fairies

The Dance Fairies

The Music Fairies

The Sports Fairies

The Party Fairies

Read them all!

■ SCHOLASTIC

www.scholastic.com
www.rainbowmagiconline.com

HIT entertainment

RMFAIRY2

RAINBOW magic

These activities are magical!
Play dress-up, send friendship notes, and much more!

SCHOLASTIC
www.scholastic.com
www.rainbowmagiconline.com

HiT entertainment

RMACTIV3